KT-569-623

Suzy was a little striped cat.
She lived in France with a fisherman who had four sons;
Pierre was ten, Henri was eight, Paul was six and Gaby was four.
When they stood in a row they looked like a set of steps.

Gaby didn't know the proper way to stroke a cat.
Most cats like being stroked from head to tail, the way the fur lies.
But Gaby always stroked Suzy backwards from tail to head
and Suzy LOVED it.

BOURNEMOUTH LIBRARIES

620007055 P

England

BOURNEMOUTH LIBRARIES

620007055 P

JF	£5.99
2006	PETERS

For Tricia and her children,
Joanna, Roderick and Caroline –
not forgetting D.H.
J.T.

For Beatrice
P.H.

France

Chez-moi (Sounds like shay-mwa)
Meaning: My home

Merci (Sounds like mare-see)
Meaning: Thank you

Au Revoir (Sounds like oh revwar)
Meaning: Goodbye

First published in this edition 2006
by Egmont UK Limited
239 Kensington High Street, London W8 6SA
The Cat who Wanted to go Home first published 1972
by Methuen & Co Ltd
Text copyright © 1972 The Estate of Jill Tomlinson
Abridgement by permission of the Estate
Illustrations © 2006 Paul Howard
Paul Howard has asserted his moral rights
ISBN-10   1 4052 0600 4 (hb)
ISBN-13   978 1 4052 0600 6 (hb)
ISBN-10   1 4052 1873 8 (pb)
ISBN-13   978 1 4052 1873 3 (pb)
1 3 5 7 9 10 8 6 4 2
All rights reserved
A CIP catalogue record for this title is available from the British Library

Printed in Italy

The Cat who Wanted to go Home

words by
Jill Tomlinson

illustrated by
Paul Howard

EGMONT

One day, Suzy found a huge basket in a field. She climbed in, settled in the shade under a stool and was soon fast asleep.

When she woke up, the basket was in the sky! There was a man with her.

"Hello, little cat," he said. "You will have to come with me to England."

Suzy didn't want to go. She wanted to stay in France with the boys.

"CHEZ-MOI!" she wailed. She wanted to go home.

So Suzy floated across the sea by balloon and landed in England with a bump. She jumped out of the basket and ran to the sea-front. How was she going to get home across all that water?

A lady took her to an old lady she knew, called Auntie Jo.

"Do you think you could look after this cat?" she said. "She must be lost."

"Of course," said Auntie Jo. "She'll be company for Biff."

Biff was Auntie Jo's new budgie who was just learning to talk. Auntie Jo put down a saucer of milk, so Suzy said 'thank you' in French: "MERCI!"

"What a funny miaow," said Auntie Jo.

"MERCI," said Biff.

"Oh, clever Biff," Auntie Jo said.

She stroked Suzy. Suzy purred, but it wasn't like home. She did miss Gaby stroking her the wrong way.

The next morning Suzy went to the beach. There was a man with a board going out to sea *towards France*! But what was this? He was coming back! Suzy ran to meet him.

"Do you want to come surfing with me?" he asked.

"CHEZ-MOI!" Suzy said.

They went out to sea and back several times before Suzy realized they were only doing it for fun. She had a lovely time even if she didn't get home to France that day.

The next morning, Suzy ran down to the sea. She saw a speedboat pulling a girl behind it. There was another girl getting ready to go. Suzy jumped on to her shoulder. The girl was not pleased.

"Get off!" she cried, but it was too late. Suzy got one paw tangled up in the girl's hair and hung on. Then their boat began to swerve.

"CHEZ-MOI!" Suzy wailed, making the girl lose her balance. A second later she and Suzy were in the water.

Suzy headed for the pier doing a catty sort of dog-paddle. The crew in the boat came back to pick up the water-skier.

"What happened to you?" asked the driver.

"It was that wretched cat!" she said. "It was all its fault."

"What cat?" said the man. "I can't see any cat."

"She's swimming. Look! She's nearly at the pier already."

Suzy climbed on to the pier. She dodged all the people and ran home. Auntie Jo rubbed her all over with a towel and gave her dinner.

"MERCI," Suzy said, cleaning her whiskers.

"You do have a funny miaow," Auntie Jo said. "But you're a funny cat altogether."

She stroked her and Suzy purred.

But she did miss Gaby stroking her the wrong way.

The next morning, Suzy ran down to the water's edge. There was a small boat and beside it was a great big man. He was a Channel Swimmer. His wife was smearing him with greasy stuff to keep him warm during his long swim. Suzy wasn't very interested until she heard somebody say, "Well, good luck, Jim! Let's hope you get to France."

It was hardly surprising that the man found a little cat swimming beside him!

Suzy held her head up with her ears folded down to keep out the water. But she began to get very tired. Then she felt herself being scooped out of the water and wrapped in a warm towel. She settled happily. Then the wind started to get up and the sea got rougher and rougher. The man found it more and more difficult to move forward. Suzy couldn't believe it when she saw him being helped into the boat, and they turned round and headed back for England.

"CHEZ-MOI!" she cried, heartbroken. "CHEZ-MOI!"

The next morning when Auntie Jo got out her tricycle, Suzy settled in the basket. Nothing Auntie Jo said or did would move her, so she cycled to the church at the top of a hill with Suzy in the basket.

Suzy could see ships! She ran down a cliff path to the big quay. A smart motor-boat was about to leave, so she jumped aboard behind a pile of rope.

The boat took an admiral to an odd sausage-shaped ship. The sailors aboard were lined up ready for inspection. The admiral strutted between them and Suzy trotted importantly behind him. The men were trying hard not to grin; it was not often that they were inspected by a tabby cat!

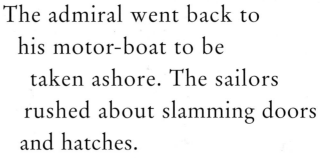

The admiral went back to
his motor-boat to be
taken ashore. The sailors
rushed about slamming doors
and hatches.
Suddenly Suzy was the only one
left. But what was happening?
The ship was sinking! Suzy
scrambled to the top of a tower-thing,
but that was sinking too!

Inside the submarine, the captain took a last look through the periscope.
"Funny!" he said. "I can't see a thing. There seems to be something
blocking it."
"Good heavens!" said the first officer. "The admiral's moggy! We'll
have to surface."

A sailor took Suzy back to the quay and she ran back to Auntie
Jo's house. Auntie Jo put some food down for Suzy.
Suzy purred. But she did miss Gaby stroking her the
wrong way.

The next morning Suzy said goodbye to Biff because she was sure she would get home to France that day.

"AU REVOIR," she said, which is French for 'goodbye'.

"AU REVOIR!" Biff said. "Clever Biff! AU REVOIR!"

Suzy and Auntie Jo pedalled down to the sea-front.

"I suppose we will see you at supper," Auntie Jo said as she went into the baker's shop. Then Suzy spotted a French sailor! She followed him to a big port. Then he turned into a large building and disappeared. Oh well. She didn't need him. One of the ships *must* be going to France.

A car drew up near Suzy.

"Is this the ferry to France?" the driver said to a man in uniform.

"That's right, sir. Just keep straight ahead," said the man.

The car joined a queue waiting to board the ferry. Suzy ran along the queue looking for a car she could get inside without being noticed. She found the very one. The boot was tied half-open with rope, leaving room for her to curl up. Suddenly there was a great clanking noise as they went down the ramp into the hold of the ship.

There was a lot of banging and clanging as people got out, slammed their car doors and disappeared through a little door in the side. At last it was quiet. Suzy squeezed between the cars and made for the door. But there was a new noise. It was the ship's engines. They were off!

Suzy hurried up some steep stairs and came out in a corridor. She went up some more stairs and came out on deck into the sunlight. She ran to the front of the ship and sat there on a curled-up rope, looking towards France.

She was going home at last.

A little girl came and sat with Suzy. "Look! Look! There's France!" she shouted.

France! Suzy could hardly believe it. Just then a sailor saw her.

"What's that cat doing there?" he asked. "She's a stowaway." He reached forward but Suzy dodged him. He chased her all around the ship and back up on deck again. Soon all the children began to join in. They thought it was a wonderful game. Poor Suzy. Nothing must stop her now.

Then Suzy saw the mast.
She ran up it and clung at the
very top. She stared around
her. France was getting nearer
and nearer – France and home.
Then she saw something else.
In the sea ahead was a French
fishing boat. And on the deck
were four little boys like steps.

It was Suzy's family!

Suzy leapt over the sailor's
head, ran to the
rail – and dived!

She seemed to go a long way down in the green water, then she came up to the surface like a cork. The children on the ferry pointed down to Suzy.

"Cat overboard!" they shouted.

The French boys saw the children were pointing to something in the sea. In a few seconds Suzy was scooped up with a bucket. The children on the ferry cheered. Suzy sat in the bucket purring like a ship's engine.

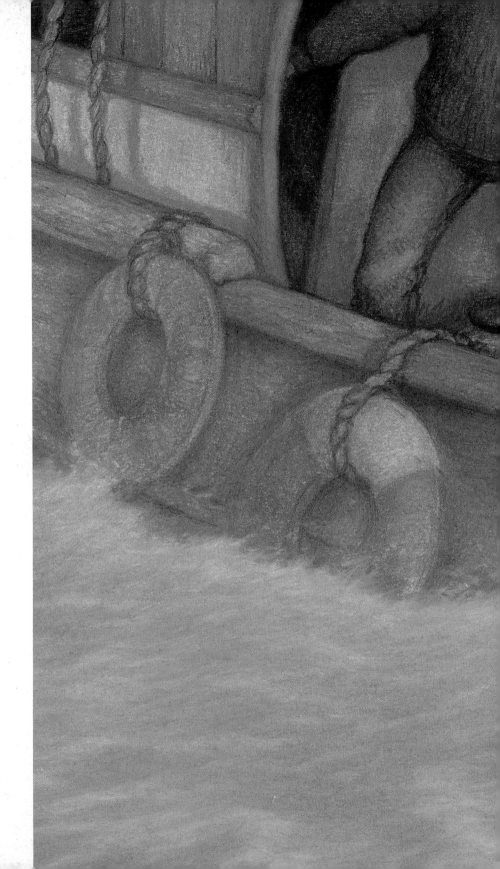

"It's Suzy!" said Gaby.
"I knew she would come back."

That evening, in England,
Auntie Jo was getting worried.
No Suzy.
"I wonder where she is?"
she said.
"Hello," said Biff.
"AU REVOIR!"
"What did you say?"
Auntie Jo said.
"Clever Biff. AU REVOIR."
"Now where did you
learn that?" said Auntie Jo.
"Of course, she
did have a
funny miaow.
I wonder . . ."

And the French cat that Auntie Jo was wondering about?
She was purring and purring as though she would never stop.
Gaby was stroking her the wrong way!

Suzy was home at last.